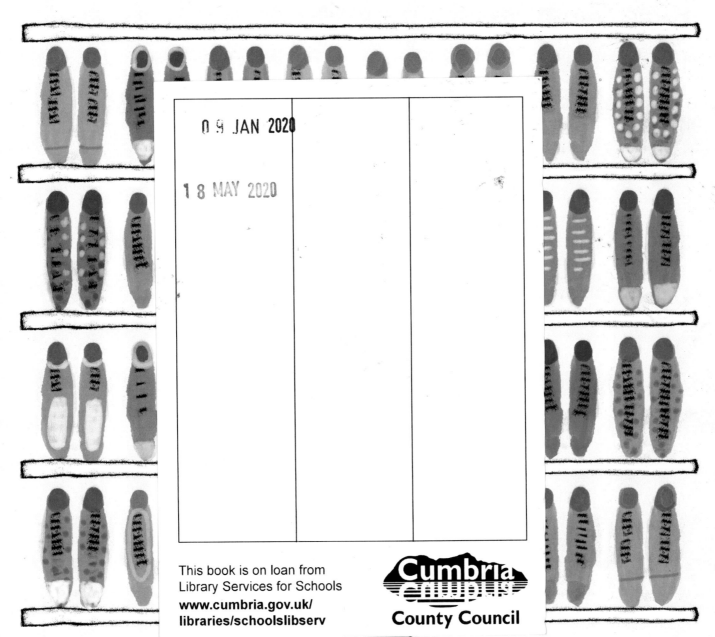

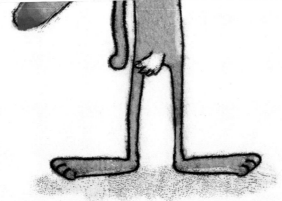

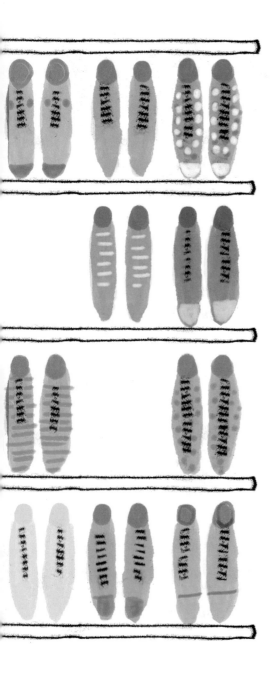

To Arthur, with love from Tim.

To Emily Ford, and all those who love cloudspotting – G. M.

First published 2019 by Macmillan Children's Books
an imprint of Pan Macmillan
20 New Wharf Road, London N1 9RR
Associated companies throughout the world
www.panmacmillan.com

ISBN 978-1-5098-8216-8 (HB)
ISBN 978-1-5098-8217-5 (PB)
ISBN 978-1-5098-8219-9 (EB)

Text copyright © Timothy Knapman 2019
Illustrations copyright © Gemma Merino 2019

Timothy Knapman and Gemma Merino have asserted their rights
to be identified as the author and illustrator of this work in accordance
with the Copyright, Designs and Patents Act 1988.

9 8 7 6 5 4 3 2 1

A CIP catalogue record for this book
is available from the British Library.

Printed in China

HARRY IN A HURRY

Timothy Knapman   Gemma Merino

MACMILLAN CHILDREN'S BOOKS

Harry was always in a hurry.

He ate fast.

He talked fast.

And he rode around and around on his scooter so fast
that everything he passed looked like this . . .

But Harry didn't care.

"Yippee!" he cried as he zoomed around, faster and faster . . .

tripping up the lollipop lady . . .

knocking over the pizza delivery boy . . .

and sending the postman – and all his letters and parcels – flying!

He didn't notice the great big hole
that he nearly fell down.

Or the prickly hedge that he nearly ran into.

Or the teeny tiny rock on the road . . .

that snagged his front wheel . . .

and sent him and his scooter flying . . .

right into the pond.

When Tom fished him out, Harry hurt all over and his scooter was bent and wobbly.

"It's broken!" said Harry. "But I'm in a hurry!"
"Where are you going?" asked Tom.
"I don't know!" said Harry. "I won't know until I get there.
And now I'm going to be late!"

Tom didn't understand, but Harry looked very upset.
"I'll fix your scooter," he said, "but it will take time."

Tom was never in a hurry.

He ate so slowly that it was lunchtime
before he'd finished his breakfast.

He talked so slowly that people fell fast asleep listening to him.

And he sneezed so slowly it took him half an afternoon to blow his nose.

"I'm sorry your scooter's taking so long to fix,"
said Tom. "Let's have some lunch.
That'll cheer you up."

Harry hated waiting more than anything!
But he hurt all over so he couldn't really
go anywhere.

Harry was grumpy. But it was strange.
Waiting for Tom, he noticed how cosy his house was,
how comfy his chair felt and how nice that soup smelled.

"Food is ready!" said Tom at long, long last.

By then, Harry was very hungry. Usually, Harry
ate as fast as he could. But he'd hurt his arm
so that, for once, he had to eat slowly.

He was still quite grumpy. But it was strange.
Eating slowly, his food tasted delicious!
And, for the very first time, it didn't give him
hiccups afterwards!

Tom spent the afternoon working on the scooter.
"I'm sorry it's taking so long to fix," he said.
"Let's go for a walk. That'll cheer you up."

Usually, Harry went everywhere as fast as he could. But he'd hurt his leg so that, for once, he had to walk slowly.

He was still a little grumpy.
But it was strange.
Walking slowly, the world around
him wasn't a big messy blur.

It was beautiful!

Tom had work to do so he
slipped away.

Harry didn't notice.
He took a deep breath . . .
and got a really good look at it all.

Harry was still there, hours later, when Tom came back with his scooter. It was as good as new.

"Thank you!" said Harry.
"I'm sorry it took so long," said Tom.

"No, *I'm* sorry!" said Harry.

"I was so grumpy! But because of you I know that a house can be cosy and food can be delicious and the world around me is beautiful! How can I ever thank you?"

For once, Tom didn't have
to think for very long.